Who is Bullying Ewe?

written and illustrated by
mandy elizabeth rush

The lambing snows arrived on the sixteenth of May
Melvaig's woolly babies were born the next day
Elder Ewe, the first born, always in a hurry
From his mum escaped in a little snow flurry

Elvis Ewe and Elfin Ewe, the twins were next born
The snow lay as a dusting that early morn
Elvis on seeing the world started to sing,
Elfin, despite the marvellous ears, couldn't yet hear a thing

Ebony Ewe, dark and glistening, slid into the world
Head over heels from her mummy she unfurled

Then she sat up, then stood up, then she
started to twirl!
For Ebony Ewe was a dancing girl

The last to be born was not a fluffy wee ball
It actually didn't look like the other ewes at all
Short hair, one horn and her face was quite long
The others exclaimed, unkindly, 'Well, you don't
belong!'

But her mummy gazed down with nothing but love
Her baby nuzzled in, they fit together like a glove
Their eyes met, their noses sniffed, their love just
grew
And they whispered to each other 'I love Ewe'

Week after week the ewes played in the burn on the
croft
They grew taller and stronger, their wool long and
soft
All except the wee ewe who looked a bit like a horse
She was forced to stay away with her Mummy in the
gorse

Equine Ewe is what she came to be called
Her treatment by the others really appalled
They were unkind and cruel only because she looked
different
Really, how they were behaving was bullying, horrid and
ignorant

At Ewe School the girls were taught how to read and write
They learned how to knit woolly jumpers that fit them tight

Counting exercises they found very easy
But fighting and boxing lessons left them queasy

One day three hungry lions into Melvaig came roaring
The flock of sheep became afraid and imploring

They rounded the ewes up, locked them away behind a
gate
And one by one, the lions hunted the ewes and they
ate

Little Equine Ewe and her mummy who were banished
from the flock
Watched the slow massacre with horror and shock
Equine Ewe was now tall, clever and strong
She decided to save the others, but she didn't have
long

The hungry lions, Richard, Edward and Henry
Pulled apart the Ewes in a bloody frenzy
Deciding who was next, they taunted and teased
The Ewes now knew that the lions couldn't be
appeased

Equine tip toed to the sheepfold one starry night
Sharing with the Ewes her plan, and why they must
fight

'These lions' she explained, 'won't leave until they have sucked your bones dry!
Lamb for breakfast, lunch and dinner and even in stir fry! '

Bellies swollen the lions slept and snored
So poison into their water Equine poured

Thirsty and hungry the lions awoke
After quenching their thirst, they started to
choke

Equine's mum took the chance to set the ewes free
The girls jumped, bounced and twirled around with glee
The lions were weakened but still they roared
Then Equine with her one horn, the lions she gored

For Equine was very different, that was true
She was a foundling baby of Mrs Mummy Ewe
Her horn is what is called a magical alicorn
Which can only be found on the unicorn

The ewes hurried forward and assisted brave Equine
Chasing the lions from their village, as they started
to whine, "Ehh!"

Further they chased, over mountain, hill and glen
Sending the lions homeward, to think again

The Ewes learnt a lesson about being unkind
And in honour of their unicorn her image they
enshrined

Before Equine, the Unicorn, all ewes bowed and bent their knee
The Unicorn, the national animal of Scotland, by King Robert's decree

The Unicorn
The national animal of Scotland

The Unicorn is the national animal of Scotland, adopted by King Robert III, grandson of King Robert the Bruce.

The Unicorn is a symbol of purity and innocence, power and strength, it is untameable and with divining truth and it can pierce the heart of a liar with its horn.

An animal that would rather die than be captured and the only animal which can defeat a lion. (Lions are the national animal of England).

Royal Coat of Arms in England

Dieu et mon driot — God and my right
The lion is the national animal of England

Two versions of the Royal Coat of arms exist in the United Kingdom of Great Britain and Northern Ireland. In Scotland the unicorn is on the left and bears a crown to show it's significance.

In England the Royal Coat of arms has the unicorn on the right and without a crown. The unicorn in both coat of arms is wrapped in chains because it is the strongest of all animals, an animal which cannot be defeated.

Royal coat of Arms in Scotland

Nemo de Impune Lacessit
No one provokes me with impunity

What Duar meddle wi me'
(No one can harm me unpunished)

We Forgive Ewe

Let's Be Friends

More books by Mandy

Scottish Beastie Books
Haggis History & Facts
Midge Myths & Facts
Puffin Parable & Facts

  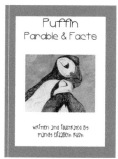

Laugh and learn as you read these beautifully illustrated books inspired by life in the remote West Highlands of Scotland.

What do Haggis eat?
Why do Midges eat you?
Who is eating Puffins and can we stop them?

Gracie MacKay is a Toothfairie's dream
For Gracie MacKay always keeps her teeth clean. . .

Nancy Coo walks 500 sMiles

Nancy Coo has lost her smile
To find it she'll search 500 mile!

Join Nancy Coo on her 500 Miles adventure around Scotland's North Coast. Visit the beautiful Highlands of Scotland and its wildlife to find out if the wee Highland Coo will find her smile.

The perfect 'travel book for those touring' the NC500 – Scotland's Route 66.

Buy Further Books at:
Web: www. mandyerush. me
Email: mandyerush@me. com

About Mandy

Mandy lives in 'The Last House before the Lighthouse' in the remote West Highlands of Scotland.

She lives with her ginger chickens, The Weasleys, Araucana Amy and four ducks, The Royal Duckesses named Sutherland, Ross, Cromarty and Fife.

Mandy loves to write and illustrate books about the wonders of the Highlands where she is surrounded by Haggis friendly habitat.

Mandy protects several secret local Haggii holts.

Dear Reader

As I, Mandy, write, illustrate and self publish all my own books. I would like to thank you, dear reader for supporting me in my passion of story telling and illustration.

It doesn't pay my bills yet but it fuels my soul.

A family of Haggii, a 'huddle', midge feasting in May in Melvaig, Wester Ross, The Highlands of Scotland

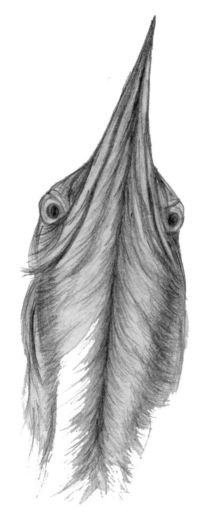

Special Thank Ewes to my dear
friend and 'spill chicker' Tracy

And to my dear friend and 'speel chicken' Margot, Thank Ewe

who is Bullying ewe?

the lions, the unicorn and the ewes

The story of Scotland's national animal, the Unicorn.

Equine, a foundling, is adopted by Mrs Ewe. She is bullied by the other ewes on the croft just because she looks different but when lions arrive and start to eat the bullies, it is brave little Equine who comes to their rescue.

who is Bullying ewe?
copyright © 2020 ♥ mandy elizabeth rush

ISBN 9781913092054

90000 >

MIX
Paper from responsible sources
FSC® C013249
www.fsc.org

9 781913 092054

printed in the uk